D. Hay Fleming

The Story of the Scotish Covenants

D. Hay Fleming

The Story of the Scotish Covenants

1st Edition | ISBN: 978-3-75240-429-6

Place of Publication: Frankfurt am Main, Germany

Year of Publication: 2020

Outlook Verlag GmbH, Germany.

Reproduction of the original.

The Story

of the

SCOTTISH COVENANTS

in Outline

by

D. Hay Fleming

SIGNING OF THE NATIONAL COVENANT IN GREYFRIARS CHURCHYARD

28th February 1638

From the Picture by W. HOLE, R.S.A.

Reproduced by permission of the Corporation of Edinburgh

and of H. E. Moss, Esq., the donor

—————————————

DESCRIPTION OF THE PROMINENT FIGURES

Beginning at the left hand is Johnston of Warriston showing a letter to the Earl of Argyll, while Lord Eglinton is in the rear. Two ladies come next—the Marchioness of Hamilton, in widow's weeds, seated, with Lady Kenmure standing beside her. The group around the tombstone includes Lord Rothes in the act of signing the document, Lord Louden, Lord Lothian, and the Earl of Sutherland; while Montrose is on the near side. Then there are Hope of Craighall, with the Rev. Samuel Rutherfurd, and in the foreground, standing on a tombstone, is the Rev. Alexander Henderson.

The Story
of the
SCOTTISH COVENANTS
in Outline

Scotland is pre-eminently the land of the Covenant, and the land is flowered with martyr graves. When the covenanting cause was in the ascendant, many were willing to appear on its side who cared little for it in reality; but when it waned, and, after the Restoration, the time of trial came, the half-hearted changed sides, or fell away like leaves in autumn, and the love of many waxed cold. Then it was that the faithful remnant stood revealed and grew still more faithful.

While they were opposed and oppressed by some of their former associates, they were, on the other hand, reinforced by the accession of outstanding men, like Richard Cameron and Thomas Forrester, who, in their earlier years, had complied with Prelacy; and by others, like James Renwick, Patrick Walker, and Sergeant Nisbet, who were born after the persecution had actually commenced. Men, and even women, were found ready and willing to endure all hardships, and to brave an ignominious death, rather than relinquish or compromise the principles which they held so dear, and to which, as they believed, the nation was bound by solemn covenants.

| Bands or Covenants |

The story of religious covenanting in Scotland covers a long period. The covenants, or bands as they were frequently called, may be divided into three classes—public, semi-public, and private—and the influence of each has been felt at some of the most critical periods in the history of the country.

| Personal Covenants |

The private or personal covenant, in which the individual Christian gave up himself, or herself, formally to the service of God, helped many a one to walk straight in crooked and trying times. These private transactions were neither less solemn nor less sacred because the knowledge of them was confined to the covenanter and his Lord.

| A Specimen |

Many specimens of these old personal covenants have been preserved, and they throw a vivid light on a type of earnest piety, which, it is to be feared, is rather rare in the present day. One of these came into my hands twenty years ago, inside a copy of Patrick Gillespie's well-known work, "The Ark of the Testament Opened." The book was printed at London in 1661, and is still in the original binding, but the old brown calf had given way at the joints, and so one of the previous owners had it rebacked. Fortunately, the binder preserved the fly-leaves, on which there are a number of jottings and dates; and on one of them there is a genuine personal covenant, written and signed by Francis Wark. He had written this covenant on that side of the last fly-leaf which was next to the board, and had then pasted the edges carefully down to the board, so that no one could see that there was any writing there. After being hidden for more than a century and a half, it was revealed by the binder. As it is very short, it may be quoted as an example:—

"I, Francis Wark, doe hereby testifie and declair that I, being a poor miserable sinner deserving hell and wrath, and that vengance is my due, and I, not being able to deliver myself from wrath nor satisfie the justice of God for my guilt, doe this day betake myself to the righteousnes of Jesws Christ, fulie renowncing all righteousnes in my self, and betakes me to his mercy; and likways that I take the true God, who made the heavns and the earth and gave me a being upon the world, to be my God and my portion (renowncing the devill the world and the flesh), and resigns up myself sowll and body to be his in tyme and through all the ages of endless eternity, even to him who is one God, Father, Son, and Holy Ghost; and I take Jesws Christ for my Saviour, my Priest, Prophet and King, and engages to be for him and his glory, whill I have a being upon the earth: in witnes quhereof I have subscrived this with my hand, Glasgow the 21 day of May 1693,

"FRANCIS WARK."

God our Portion

Documents of this kind help one to understand the reply of the covenanter's wife when the dragoons were driving away all the cattle in her husband's absence. A soldier, who had not altogether lost his feelings of humanity, turned back to her and said: "Puir woman, I'm sorry for you." "Puir!" she exclaimed, "I'm no puir; the Lord is my portion, and ye canna mak me puir!"

There is still some uncertainty as to the precise date when public or semi-public religious covenanting was adopted in Scotland.

Supposed Band of 1556

In speaking of his own preaching in 1556, Knox tells that, at that time, most of the gentlemen of the Mearns "refuissed all societie with idolatrie, and

5

band thame selfis, to the uttermost of thare poweris, to manteane the trew preaching of the Evangell of Jesus Christ, as God should offer unto thame preachearis and oportunitie." Dr M'Crie understood this to mean that these gentlemen "entered into a solemn and mutual bond, in which they renounced the Popish communion, and engaged to maintain and promote the pure preaching of the Gospel, as Providence should favour them with opportunities." In David Laing's opinion, Knox's words do not necessarily imply that the mutual agreement or resolution referred to actually assumed the form of a written "band" or covenant. If it did, Knox has not embodied it in his "History," nor is any copy known to exist.

Band of 1557   But as to the reality, the nature, and the precise date of the band of 1557, there is no room for dubiety. Knox was on the Continent when it was entered into; but he relates the circumstances which called it forth, explains the object it was meant to serve, and gives a copy of the document itself, as well as the names of the principal men who signed it. The leaders of the Reforming party resolved to persist in their purpose, to commit themselves and their all into God's hands, rather than allow idolatry manifestly to reign, rather than suffer the subjects of the realm to be defrauded as they had been of the preaching of Christ's Evangel. "And that everie ane should be the more assured of other, a commoun band was maid, and by some subscrived."

Calderwood derived his copy of the document, and his account of the circumstances which called it forth, from Knox. Fully forty years ago an original copy of the band was found, and is now in the National Museum of Antiquities, Edinburgh. It only bears five signatures, those of Argyll, Glencairn, Morton, Lorne, and John Erskine. The day of the month is left blank; but the one which Knox followed is dated "the thrid day of December." Knox also says that it was subscribed by many others. The explanation probably is that (as in 1638) a number of original copies were made, and signed by the leaders before being sent out for additional names.

This band of 1557, like those of a later date, is remarkable for the clearness, the directness, and the vigour of its language, but unlike them it can hardly be regarded as a public document. To have exhibited it then to all and sundry would have been to court persecution, perhaps death. "To those who agreed with them," says Buchanan, "they presented bonds for their subscription. These first assumed the name of 'the Congregation,' which those who followed afterward rendered more celebrated." Although there are barely two hundred and fifty words in the band of 1557, the Protestant party is mentioned in it seven times as the Congregation. It was nearly five months after the date of this band before Walter Mill was consigned to the flames.

The year 1559 was rendered notable in Scotland by the return of Knox, by the open rupture between the Congregation and the Queen Regent, and by the rapid progress of Protestantism. In the summer of that year the Reformers deemed it advisable to enter into at least three distinct covenants, their respective dates being the 31st of May, the 13th of July, and the 1st of August. None of the originals of these is known to have survived, but copies of all the three have been preserved. They had for their general object the advancement of the Reformation, but each had its own distinctive traits and special end. The first was entered into at Perth, the second at Edinburgh, and the third at Stirling. The second was adopted in St Andrews as the "letteris of junctioun to the Congregatioun," and as such was taken by more than three hundred persons.

Rupture of French Alliance Not the least striking result of the Reformation was the complete bursting up of the ancient alliance between France and Scotland, and the drawing together of Scotland and England—that England which Scotland had so long and so recently regarded as its "auld enemy." The importance of this result is frankly acknowledged by Teulet, one of the most competent, careful, and candid of French historical students. He puts the matter thus: "Scotland, which was for so many ages the devoted ally of France, the rein, as our ancient kings said, with which they restrained the encroachments of England, was unwilling to abdicate its nationality and become a French province. Moreover, the unbridled excesses of the French troops in Scotland, no less than the shameless rapacity of the French agents, at last aroused a general spirit of resistance, and England soon found in the rupture of the ancient alliance between France and Scotland an ample indemnification for the loss of Calais."

French Excesses The enormities of the French in Scotland were so great, that Mary of Guise, in writing to her brothers, affirmed that the peasantry were in consequence so reduced to despair that they frequently committed suicide. Although these unbridled excesses are enough to explain the revulsion of feeling towards the French, they do not quite account for the sudden alteration towards the English. The change, indeed, was so sudden and so unlikely that some Southerns thought, and naturally thought, it was "a traine to betrappe" their nation.

Scots and English So great had been the Scotch hatred of the English, that, from the French who came over to help them after Pinkie, they were said to have bought English prisoners, that they might have the pleasure of putting them to death, although they could ill afford the price which they paid ungrudgingly. This hatred, so bitter, so fierce, and so recent, could not have been wiped out by any French oppression had not the Scots been now finding themselves ranged on the same side as the English in the great religious struggle, which was submerging old feuds, breaking up old compacts, and turning the world upside down.

Band of 1560 The oppression by the French, and the help expected from the English army, are both referred to in the band or covenant entered into on the 27th of April 1560. Knox says that this band was made by "all the nobilitie, barronis, and gentilmen, professing Chryst Jesus in Scotland," and by "dyveris utheris that joynit with us, for expelling of the Frenche army; amangis quham the Erle of Huntlie was principall." He does not name any other person who signed, although he copied the band itself into his "History"; but the original document was found among the Hamilton MSS., and it bears about a hundred and fifty signatures of noblemen and gentlemen, including those of the Duke of Chatelherault, the Earls of Arran, Huntly, Argyll, Glencairn, Rothes, and Morton, James Stewart (afterwards the Regent Murray), and the Abbots of Kinloss, Coupar, and Kilwinning. All those who adhibited their names did not do so on the same day. Huntly signed on the 28th of April; Morton and twenty-seven others on the 6th of May.

Treaty of Edinburgh The French had fortified Leith, but were so hard pressed by the English and the Scots that they were constrained to make the Treaty of Edinburgh, with Queen Elizabeth's representatives, on the 6th of July 1560. It was by that treaty, or rather—to be more strictly accurate—in virtue of the concessions in the separate "accord" between the French and the Scots of the same date, and which is referred to in the treaty, that the Scots were able to throw off for ever the merciless tyranny of their old allies and the unbearable yoke of the Papacy. These concessions provided for a meeting of Parliament; and next month that Parliament repealed the Acts favouring the Church of Rome, abolished the Pope's jurisdiction in Scotland, prohibited the celebration of mass under pain of death for the third conviction, and ratified the Confession of Faith drawn up by Knox, Wynram, Spottiswoode, Willock, Douglas, and Row.

Mary Queen of Scots returned from France to her own country in August 1561, and a year later made her first northern progress, in which she went as far as Inverness. Huntly, notwithstanding his having signed the band of 1560, was regarded as the lay head of the Papists in Scotland, and grave doubts were entertained by many of the Protestants as to the results of this progress of the young Queen.

Band of 1562 Knox was then in Ayrshire, and, alarmed by the rumours which reached him, he prevailed on many of the barons and gentlemen of that county to enter into another band, or covenant, at Ayr, on the 4th of September 1562, in order to be prepared for any attempt that might be made to put down Protestantism. It does not appear that it had any influence on the course of events in the North, but it probably had a considerable, though indirect, influence in restraining those in the South, who might have been inclined to help Huntly had there been any prospect of their being able to do so successfully. Those who took the band were not called upon to show their faithfulness in the field. Huntly—through perversity, stupidity, or suspicion—put himself completely out of the Queen's graces. His forces were defeated, he died on the field of battle, one of his sons was executed, and another imprisoned.

The Queen's Demission On Thursday, the 24th of July 1567, the Queen, then a prisoner in Loch Leven Castle, was prevailed upon (by threats, she afterwards said) to demit the government in favour of her infant son, James, then thirteen months old. The General Assembly had met on the preceding Monday in the Over Tolbooth of Edinburgh; and on Friday, the 25th, the nobles, barons, and commissioners of towns, who were present, agreed to and subscribed certain "articles."

Articles of 1567 These articles really formed a band for subverting the mass, destroying monuments of idolatry, setting up the true religion through the whole realm, increasing ministers' stipends, reforming schools, colleges, and universities, easing the poor of their teinds, punishing vice, crimes, and offences, especially the murder of Darnley, defending the young prince, bringing him up in the fear of God, and obliging future kings and rulers to promise, before their coronation and inauguration, to maintain, defend, and set forward, the true religion. The subscribers also consented and offered "to reforme themselves according to the Booke of God." In all they numbered about eighty. Of these, two or three certainly knew of the plot against Darnley before it was carried out; and they may have subscribed these articles to avert suspicion.

St Bartholomew's Massacre The dreadful massacre of the Huguenots, begun in Paris on St Bartholomew's day 1572, excited consternation and horror in Scotland. Believing that all the other Protestants in Europe were to be similarly dealt with, the Privy Council summoned a convention, to be held at Edinburgh on the 20th of October, to consider the impending danger and the means by which it might be averted. Unfortunately for the success of the convention, the lieges had been summoned to meet at Jedburgh on the 22nd to make a raid upon the border thieves; and the Earl of Mar, then Regent, was drawing near his end at Stirling. None of the nobles and few of the lairds attended the convention; but

Proposed Band

a number of proposals were agreed to, that they might be sent to the Regent and the Privy Council. One of these proposals was that a public humiliation, or fast, should be held throughout the whole of Scotland during the last eight days of November. Another was that the Protestants of the realm should enter into a solemn band, that they might be ready on all occasions to resist the enemy. There is evidence to show that the fast was observed in Edinburgh; but, if the band was ever drawn up, no copy of it seems to have survived, nor any record of its having been entered into. The suggestion, however, was not fruitless. In the following January,

| Test Of Loyalty | Parliament enacted that no one should be reputed a loyal subject to the King, but should be punished as a rebel, who did not profess the true religion; and that those who had made profession thereof, and yet had departed from their due obedience to his Majesty, should not be received to his mercy and favour, until they anew gave confession of their faith; and promised to continue "in the confessioun of the trew religioun" in time coming, and to maintain the King's authority; and also that they would, "at the uttermest of thair power, fortifie, assist and mantene the trew preichouris and professouris of Christis religioun," against all enemies and gainstanders of the same, of whatever nation, estate, or degree, who had bound themselves, or assisted, to set forward and execute the cruel decrees of the Council of Trent, injuriously called, by the adversaries of God's truth, "The Haly League." By this time the "Tulchan Bishops" had been obtruded on the Church of Scotland.

| The King's Confession | All the earlier covenants were eclipsed in interest and importance by the one drawn up by John Craig, and commonly called "The King's Confession," sometimes "The Second Confession of Faith," and sometimes "The Negative Confession." In it the corruptions of the Papacy are denounced and renounced in terse language and with refreshing vigour. As John Row puts it: "This wes the touch-stone to try and discern Papists from Protestants." And yet, notwithstanding its searching and solemn words, it failed in at least one notable instance as a touch-stone. The original document, signed by James the Sixth and his household on the 28th of January 1580-81, found its way to France, but fortunately was sent back again to this country—to Scot of Scotstarvit—and is now in the Advocates' Library. This covenant was subscribed in 1581 by all ranks and classes of the people.

Because of "the great dangers which appeared to hang over the kirk and countrie," a special meeting of the General Assembly was convened on the 6th of February 1587-8. In the fifteenth session, it was agreed that ministers should "travell diligentlie with the noblemen, barons, and gentlemen, to subscribe the Confession of Faith." In accordance with this resolution, the

Negative Confession was again signed by the King, and nearly a hundred other persons, including several of the leading nobles, on the 25th of February, at Holyrood.

| The General Band | The dread inspired by the approach of the Spanish Armada in 1588 led to the preparation of another covenant, known as "The General Band." The subscribers did "solemnly swear and promise to take a true, effald and plain parte with his Majestie amongst ourselves, for diverting of the present danger threatned to the said [true and Christian] religion, and his Majestie's estate and standing depending thereupon." There is record evidence to show that it was subscribed by the King "and divers of his Esteatis" before the 27th of July 1588.

| Band of 1589 | This was a time of special bands. At Aberdeen, on the 30th of April 1589, the King and many others subscribed a band, by which they bound themselves together "for the defens and suretie of the said trew religioun, his Hienes persone and estate thairwith conjoynit"; and for the pursuit of "Jesuittis, Papistis of all sortis, thair assistaris and pairttakaris," including the Earls of Huntly and Errol, who had "cum to the feildis with oppin and plane force and displayit baner, for the persute, ruting-oute and exterminioun of his Majestie, and all uthiris his gude and loving subjectis, trew professouris of the Evangell."

| Covenanting in 1590 | On the 6th of March 1589-90, when King James was still beyond the German Ocean with his bride, the Privy Council, frightened again by the rumours of a foreign invasion, appointed commissioners to receive the subscriptions of nobles, barons, gentlemen, and lieges of every degree, to the King's Confession of 1580-81, and to the General Band of 1588. Robert Waldegrave was authorised to print these documents for that special purpose; and they were issued by him, in 1590, in book form, with blank pages after the Confession, and also after the General Band, for signatures. The subscribing at this time is said to have been universal.

| Band of 1592-3 | The discovery, in December 1592, of the documents known as the Spanish Blanks, led to another royal expedition to the North in the following February. While in Aberdeen, the King, several of his nobles, and about a hundred and fifty of the prominent lairds, entered into another band. It proceeds on the narrative that, being fully and certainly persuaded of the treasonable practices and conspiracies of some of his subjects, against "the estat of the true religioun presentlie professed within this realme, his Majestie's person, crowne, and libertie of this our native countrie," the subscribers faithfully bind and oblige themselves "to concurre, and take an effald, leill, and true part with his Majestie, and each

one of us with others, to the maintenance and defence of the libertie of the said true religioun, crown, and countrie, from thraldom of conscience, conqueist, and slaverie of strangers, and [in] resisting, repressing, and pursute of the cheefe authors of the saids treasonable conspiraceis."

The precise date of this band is not given, but it must have been subscribed between the 1st and the 13th of March 1592-3, that is, in 1592 according to the old reckoning by which the year began on the 25th of March, but in 1593 according to the present reckoning by which the year begins on the 1st of January.

| Covenanting in 1596 | In March 1596, the General Assembly, anxious "to see the Kirk and ministrie purged," determined to humble itself for the short-comings and corruptions of the ministry, and resolved that a new covenant should be made with God, "for a more carefull and reverent discharge of their ministrie." Accordingly, on Tuesday the 30th, "foure hundreth persons, all ministers or choice professors," met in the Little Kirk of Edinburgh, and there entered into "a new league with God," promising "to walke more warilie in their wayes and more diligentlie in their charges." While humbling themselves, "there were suche sighes and sobbs, with shedding of teares among the most part of all estats that were present, everie one provoking another by their exemple, and the teacher himself [John Davidson] by his exemple, that the kirk resounded, so that the place might

| Bochim | worthilie have beene called Bochim; for the like of that day was never seene in Scotland since the Reformatioun." As a great many of the ministers were not present at this action, it was ordered to be repeated in the synods, and in presbyteries by those who were absent from their synod. It was likewise taken up in parishes. In the Presbytery of St Andrews, "for testefeing of a trew conversioun and change of mynd," special promises and vows were made. These referred to religious duties, in private, in the family, and in public, including "the resisting of all enemies of relligioun, without fear or favour of anie persone"; and also referred to such ordinary duties, as taking order with the poor, and repairing bridges.[1]

---

1. Row and the younger M'Crie are apparently in error in stating that the covenant of 1580-81 was renewed in 1596. Long before that time, however, it had been assigned a place in the Book of Laureations of Edinburgh University, that it might be subscribed by the professors and students.

| Erection of Episcopacy | James the Sixth's hankering for Prelacy and its ritual continued to increase after he crossed the Tweed in 1603. By the summer of 1610, "the restoration of

episcopal government and the civil rights of bishops" had been accomplished; but, according to the best-informed of Scottish Episcopalian historians, "there was yet wanting that without which, so far as the Church was concerned, all the rest was comparatively unimportant." The Archbishop of Glasgow, and the Bishops of Brechin and Galloway, were sent up, however, to the English court, and on the 21st of October "were consecrated according to the form in the English ordinal." This qualified them on their return to give "valid ordination" to the Archbishop of St Andrews (George Gladstanes) and the other bishops. Gladstanes seems to have felt duly grateful to the King, whom he addressed as his "earthly creator." The Court of High Commission had already been erected; and in 1612 Parliament formally rescinded the Act of 1592, regarded as the charter of Presbytery. A General Assembly held at

| Articles of Perth | Perth, in August 1618, agreed by a majority to the five articles, afterwards known as "the Articles of Perth"; and they were ratified by Parliament in August 1621.[2]

2. By the five articles of Perth—

(1) Kneeling at the Lord's Supper was approved;

(2) Ministers were to dispense that sacrament in private houses, to those suffering from infirmity or from long or deadly sickness;

(3) Ministers were to baptise children in private houses in cases of great need;

(4) Ministers were, under pain of the bishop's censure, to catechise all children of eight years of age, and the children were to be presented to the bishop for his blessing;

(5) Ministers were ordered to commemorate Christ's birth, passion, resurrection, ascension, and the sending down of the Holy Ghost.

| Revolt of 1637 | When Charles the First ascended the throne, in 1625, he found that the northern church still lagged behind its southern sister. He resolved to supply the defects, and the projects which he laid for this purpose had a considerable influence on the events which subsequently brought him to the block. Had he shown more caution and less haste, he might possibly have succeeded in his attempts on the Scottish Church; but in Laud he had an evil adviser. The storm burst in the High Church (St Giles) of Edinburgh, when Dean Hanna tried to read the new liturgy, on the 23rd of July 1637. With this tumult the name of Jenny Geddes has been associated. The Presbyterian party, so long down-trodden, began to

assert their rights; and, finding that they would be better able to withstand opposition if closely bound together, they determined to fall back on the plan of their ancestors by entering into a solemn covenant.

As the basis of this covenant the King's Confession of 1580-81 was chosen, and to it two additions were made, the first, prepared by Archibald Johnston of Warriston, is known as "the legal warrant," and the second, drawn up by Alexander Henderson of Leuchars, was the bond suiting it to the occasion.

| National Covenant | With these additions it was, and still is, known as "The National Covenant"; and in that form it was sworn to and subscribed by thousands of people, in Greyfriars Church and churchyard, on the 28th of February 1638, and by hundreds of ministers and commissioners of burghs next day. Copies were sent all over the country, and were readily signed in almost every district. The enthusiasm was unbounded. The King could not prevail on the swearers to resile from their position, and therefore tried to sow dissension among them by introducing a rival covenant. For this purpose he likewise selected the King's Confession of 1580-81; but instead of Johnston's and Henderson's additions, he substituted the General Band of 1588; and so the two documents combined in 1590 were again brought together. This attempt to divide the Covenanters utterly failed. The people now called the covenant completed by Johnston and Henderson, "The Noblemen's Covenant"; and the one sent out by Charles, "The King's Covenant."

| Glasgow Assembly | The General Assembly which met at Glasgow on the 21st of November 1638 was dissolved by the Royal Commissioner; but Henderson, who was moderator, pointed to the Commissioner's zeal for an earthly king as an incentive to the members to show their devotion to the cause of their heavenly King; and the Assembly continued to sit until it had condemned and annulled the six General Assemblies held between 1606 and 1618, and had made a clean sweep of the bishops, their jurisdiction, and their ceremonies.

Next summer Charles marched with an English army into Scotland, only to find a strong force of Covenanters, under Alexander Leslie, encamped on Duns Law. Deeming discretion the better part of valour, the King entered into negotiations, and the Treaty of Berwick followed. By it he agreed that a General Assembly should be held in August, and thereafter a Parliament to ratify its proceedings. The Assembly met, and by an Act enjoined all professors and schoolmasters, and all students "at the passing of their degrees," to subscribe the Covenant. By another Act it rejected the service-book, the book of canons, the High Commission, Prelacy, and the ceremonies. Parliament duly met, but was prevented from ratifying the Acts of Assembly

14

by the Royal Commissioner, who adjourned it from time to time, and finally prorogued it until June 1640.

Assembly of 1639 As that time drew nigh, the King tried again to postpone or prorogue it; but it nevertheless met, and in the space of a few days effected a revolution unexampled in the previous history of Scotland. It set bounds to the power of the monarch. It ratified the Covenant, enjoining its subscription "under all civill paines"; it ratified the Act of the General Assembly of 1639, rejecting the service-book, Prelacy, etc.; it renewed the Act of Parliament of 1592 in favour of Presbytery, and annulled the Act of 1612 by which the Act of 1592 had been rescinded.

Parliament of 1640 The King had been preparing for the Second Bishops' War, and the Covenanters marched into England, Montrose being the first to cross the Tweed. Again there were negotiations, and an agreement was at length come to at Westminster in August 1641. Charles now set out for Holyrood, and in the Scottish Parliament ratified the Westminster Treaty; and so explicitly, if not cordially, approved of the proceedings of the Parliament of 1640.

The Scots had now got all that they wanted from their King, although many of them must have doubted his sincerity, and feared a future revocation should that ever be in his power. This fear, coupled with a fellow-feeling for the Puritans, and gratitude for the seasonable assistance of the English in 1560, accounts for the readiness of the compliance with the proposal of the Commissioners of the Long Parliament who arrived in Edinburgh in August 1643.

The English ask Help These Commissioners desired help from the Convention of Estates and from the General Assembly, and proposed that the two nations should enter into "a strict union and league," with the object of bringing them closer in church government, and eventually extirpating Popery and Prelacy from the island.

Solemn League and Covenant The suggestion that the league should be religious as well as civil having been accepted, Henderson drafted the famous Solemn League and Covenant.[3]
It was approved by the Convention of Estates and by the General Assembly on the 17th of August; and (after several alterations) by the Westminster Assembly and both Houses of the English Parliament.

---

3. An international Protestant league was not a new idea. The Convention, which met at Edinburgh on the 20th of October 1572, had suggested

15

that a league and confederacy should be made "with our nychtbouris of Ingland and uther cuntries reformit and professing the trew religioun," that we and they be joined together in mutual amity and society to support each other, when time or occasion shall serve, "for mantenance of religioun and resisting of the enemies thairof." In 1585, the Scottish Parliament (understanding that divers princes and potentates had joined themselves, "under the Pape's auctoritie, in a maist unchristiane confederacie, aganis the trew religioun and professouris thairof, with full intent to prosecute thair ungodlie resolutioun with all severitie") authorised the making of a Christian league with the Queen of England, to be, in matters of religion, both offensive and defensive, even against "auld freindis and confederatis." The league, or treaty, was finally concluded by commissioners, at Berwick-on-Tweed, on the 5th of July 1586.

<table>
<tr><td>

The Covenant enjoined

</td><td>

In October the Commission of the General Assembly ordered that it should be forthwith printed, and gave instructions for the swearing and subscribing,

</td></tr>
</table>

presbyteries being ordered to proceed with the censures of the kirk "against all such as shall refuse or shift to swear and subscribe"; and the Commissioners of the Convention ordained that it should be sworn by all his Majesty's Scottish subjects under pain of being "esteemed and punished as enemyes to religioune, his Majestie's honour, and peace of thir kingdomes." In Scotland it evoked more enthusiasm than in England; and, for a time at least, produced marvellous unanimity.

<table>
<tr><td>

Montrose's Army

</td><td>

The Scots took part against the royal army in the battle of Marston Moor (2nd July 1644); and soon

</td></tr>
</table>

afterwards Montrose, who had not approved of the Solemn League and Covenant, made his way into Scotland with the object of creating a diversion in favour of the King. Having raised an army in the Highlands, which was strengthened by an Irish contingent, he won a series of brilliant victories over the Covenanters at Tippermuir, Aberdeen, Inverlochy, Auldearn, Alford, and Kilsyth.

Of Montrose's army, Patrick Gordon, a royalist, wrote: "When God had given there enemies into there handes, the Irishes in particulare ware too cruell; for it was everiewhere observed they did ordinarely kill all they could be maister of, without any motion of pitie, or any consideration of humanitie: ney, it seemed to them there was no distinction betuixt a man and a beast; for they killed men ordinarly with no more feilling of compassion, and with the same carelesse neglect that they kill ane henn or capone for ther supper. And they were also, without all shame, most brutishlie given to uncleannes and filthie lust; as for excessive drinkeing, when they came where it might be had, there was no limites to there beastly appetites; as for godlesse avarice, and mercilesse oppression and plundering or the poore laborer, of those two cryeing sinnes the Scotes ware alse giltie as they."

| Retaliation |

The same writer tells how the Irish were repaid for their cruelty by the victorious army of David Leslie at and after the battle of Philiphaugh (13th September 1645); and how their sin was then visited, not only upon themselves, but most brutally and pitilessly upon their wives and followers.[4]

---

4. The various accounts of the slaughter are rather contradictory in their details. It may be noted, too, that—while Patrick Gordon says that fifty Irishmen were promised safe quarter and yet were killed—it was urged, in defence of the four prisoners condemned by the Scottish Parliament, that the quarter they had received was not against the orders of the Commander-in-Chief at Philiphaugh, as he only forbade the giving of quarter to the Irish. Nearly a year before (24th October 1644) the English Parliament had declared that "no quarter shall be given hereafter to any Irishman, nor to any Papist whatever born in Ireland, which shall be taken in hostility against the Parliament," either on the sea or in England or in Wales; and ordained that they should be excepted "out of all capitulations, agreements or compositions," and when taken should be forthwith put to death. The massacres of 1641-1642 had not been forgotten.

| The Engagement |

On the 26th of December 1647, when the King was in Carisbrooke Castle, in the Isle of Wight, he entered into an agreement in presence of three Scottish Commissioners— Loudoun, Lauderdale, and Lanark—in which he intimated his willingness to confirm the Solemn League and Covenant, by Act of Parliament in both kingdoms, provided that no one who was unwilling to take it should be constrained to do so; he was also to confirm by Act of Parliament in England, for three years, presbyterial government and the Westminster Assembly's Directory for Worship, provided that he and his household should not be hindered from using the service he had formerly practised; and further, an effectual course was to be taken by Parliament and otherwise for suppressing the opinions and practices of Anti-Trinitarians, Anabaptists, Antinomians, Arminians, Familists, Brownists, Separatists, Independents, Libertines, and Seekers.

On the other hand, Scotland was, in a peaceable way, to endeavour that the King should be allowed to go to London in safety, honour, and freedom, there to treat personally with the English Parliament and the Scottish Commissioners; and should this not be granted, Scotland was to emit certain declarations, and send an army into England for the preservation and establishment of religion, for the defence of his Majesty's person and authority, for his restoration to power, and for settling a lasting peace.

This agreement was known as "The Engagement"; and the same name was applied to the expedition which, in furtherance of its object, the Duke of Hamilton led into England, only to be crushed by Cromwell at Preston in August 1648.

Charles II. proclaimed King

The Scottish Commissioners in London did what they could to prevent the execution of Charles the First, and on the 5th of February 1649—six days after the scene in front of Whitehall—the Parliament of Scotland caused his son to be proclaimed at the Market Cross of Edinburgh, as King of Great Britain, France, and Ireland. The Scots were determined that he should be their King, but they were as determined that he should not override either the General Assembly or the Parliament.

He did not like their conditions, and the first negotiations were abortive.

Montrose organised another expedition, which collapsed at Carbisdale on the 27th of April 1650; and on the 21st of May the gallant Marquis was ignominiously hanged at the Market Cross of Edinburgh, and his dismembered body buried among malefactors in the Burgh Muir.

King and Covenants

The Prince had "already endeavoured to procure assistance from the Emperour, and the Electours, Princes, and States of the Empire, from the Kings of Spaine, France, and Denmarke, and most of the Princes and States of Italy," and had only obtained "dilatory and generall answeres." All his friends, he said, advised him "to make an agreement upon any termes with our subjects of Scotland"; and he took their advice as the only means of obtaining this crown and recovering his other kingdoms. He offered to subscribe and swear the National Covenant, and the Solemn League and Covenant, before landing at the mouth of the Spey, and he accordingly did so on the 23rd of June 1650.

On the 16th of August he agreed to the Dunfermline Declaration, deploring his father's opposition to the work of reformation, confessing his mother's idolatry, professing his own sincerity, declaring that "he will have no enemies but the enemies of the Covenant, and that he will have no friends but the friends of the Covenant," and expressing his detestation of "all Popery, superstition, and idolatry, together with Prelacy, and all errors, heresie, schism and profaneness," which he was resolved not to tolerate in any part of his dominions.

Dunbar and Scone   Notwithstanding Cromwell's notable victory at Dunbar on the 3rd of September, and the dissatisfaction of the more rigid Covenanters, now known as Remonstrants, Charles was crowned at Scone on the 1st of January 1651, when he again swore and subscribed the National Covenant, and also the Solemn League and Covenant. The Marquis of Argyll placed the crown on his head, and Robert Douglas preached the sermon. The attempt to counteract Cromwell's power in Scotland by an invasion of England was unsuccessful. The Committee of the Scottish Estates was captured at Alyth before the end of August; and Cromwell obtained his "crowning mercy" at Worcester on the 3rd of September. The young King, after many adventures and narrow escapes, was glad to find himself again on the Continent.

Resolutioners and Protesters   In December 1650, after obtaining the opinion of the Commissioners of the General Assembly, the Scottish Parliament had "admitted manie, who were formerlie excluded, to be imployed in the armie"; and in June 1651 had rescinded the Acts of Classes, by which certain classes of delinquents had been shut out of places of public trust. Those who were in favour of admitting these men were known as Resolutioners; and their opponents, as Protesters. This unfortunate dispute split the Presbyterians into two sections, and their contentions had not come to an end when the Restoration of Charles was effected in 1660.

The Restoration   That Restoration was mainly brought about by General Monk. When it was seen to be inevitable, the leading Resolutioners sent James Sharp, minister of Crail, to London, to look after the interests of the Scottish Church. He was diplomatic and astute, and, in the opinion of his brethren, honest and trustworthy. His letters, bristling with devotional expressions, "seem," as Hugh Miller puts it, "as if strewed over with the fragments of broken doxologies." After it was too late, they found that he had betrayed his trust, and completely hoodwinked them.

The King's Honour   The General Assembly had been suppressed under Cromwell's iron rule, and the Church of Scotland was otherwise handicapped at this period; but something effective might have been done to safeguard her rights had the Resolutioners not been deceived by Sharp, although it would have been impossible to make Charles the Second safe, either by the renewal of former or by additional obligations, even if the Scots had been able to impose these upon him. Such a man could not be tied by oaths. At his Restoration, those in power trusted to his honour, and of that virtue he had wondrously little.

His entry into London had been timed to take place on the 29th of May 1660 —the thirtieth anniversary of his birthday. Some of the leading Protesters, fearing the overthrow of Presbytery, met in Edinburgh, on the 23rd of August, to draw up a supplication to the King. The Committee of Estates arrested them, and imprisoned them in the castle.

| The Act Rescissory | A few days afterwards Sharp brought a letter from his Majesty, in which he said: "We do also resolve to protect and preserve the government of the Church of Scotland, *as it is settled by law*, without violation." A suggestion that this might be understood in two ways, was condemned as "an intolerable reflection" on the King. The Scottish Parliament, on the 28th of March 1661, rescinded the Parliaments which had been held in and since 1640, and all the Acts passed by them. Thus all the civil sanction which had been given to the Second Reformation was swept away at a stroke. Early next morning, Samuel Rutherfurd—whose stipend had been confiscated, whose "Lex Rex" had been burned, and who had been cited to answer a charge of treason—appeared before a court that was higher than any Parliament, and "where his Judge was his friend."

A month after this, Sharp professed, in a letter to James Wood, that he was still hopeful that there would, "through the goodnes of God," be no change; and affirmed that, as he had, "through the Lord's mercy," done nothing to the prejudice of the liberties and government of the Church, so he would not, "by the grace of God," have any accession to the wronging of it.

| Duplicity | He was then on the eve of setting out for London with Glencairn and Rothes. They returned in the end of August, bringing with them a letter intimating the King's determination to interpose his royal authority for restoring the Church of Scotland "to its right government by bishops as it was by law before the late troubles"; and justifying his action by his promise of the previous year. Candid Episcopalians admit that this dealing shook all confidence in the sincerity of Charles.

| Episcopacy Re-established | In October Sharp again went to England; in November he was appointed Archbishop of St Andrews; and in December he was consecrated in Westminster Abbey, after being privately ordained as a deacon and a priest. The Scottish Parliament, on the 27th of May 1662, passed the "Act for the restitution and re-establishment of the antient government of the church by archbishops and bishops." The preamble of this Act acknowledges that "the ordering and disposall of the externall government and policie of the Church doth propperlie belong unto his Majestie, as are inherent right of the Croun, by vertew of his royall prerogative and supremacie in causes ecclesiasticall." The Oath of Allegiance, which had been adopted by Parliament on the 1st of

January 1661, contained the clause: "I acknowledge my said Soverane only supream governour of this kingdome over all persons and in all causes."

Argyll and Guthrie The Solemn League and Covenant had already been burned by the hangman in London; and the long and bloody persecution in Scotland had already begun. An example had been made of the Marquis of Argyll, and of James Guthrie, the minister of Stirling. Both suffered at the Market Cross of Edinburgh in the same week, Argyll on Monday, the 27th of May, and Guthrie on Saturday, the 1st of June, 1661. To secure Argyll's conviction, Monk was base enough to give up several of his letters proving his hearty compliance with the Usurper's government after it was established. The case for the prosecution was closed before the letters arrived; but they were nevertheless received and read.

Sir George Mackenzie—later to acquire an unenviable notoriety as the Bluidy Mackenyie—was one of his advocates, and in his opinion the Marquis suffered mainly for the good old cause. Guthrie had never compromised himself in any way with Cromwell, who described him as the little man who would not bow.

Ministers Disqualified The Parliament of 1662 not only re-established Prelacy, but decreed that no minister, who had entered after the abolition of patronage in 1649, should have any right to his stipend unless he obtained presentation from the patron and collation from the bishop; and that ministers who did not observe the Act of 1661, appointing the day of the King's restoration as an annual holy day unto the Lord, should be incapable of enjoying any benefice. It also declared that the Covenants were unlawful oaths, and enacted that no one should be admitted to any public trust or office until he acknowledged in writing that they were unlawful.

Ministers Ejected These Acts of Parliament were speedily followed up by the Privy Council, which, in September 1662, ordered all ministers to resort next month to their respective bishop's assemblies; and in October commanded all the ministers entered since 1649, and who had not since received the patron's presentation and the bishop's collation, to quit their parishes. By this latter Act it has been reckoned that fully three hundred ministers were turned out of their charges.

Church-Courts Discharged When Prelacy was established in 1610, James the Sixth was much too politic to close the ecclesiastical courts which had been set up and carried on by the Presbyterians. "Honest men" continued to maintain in them "both their right and possession, except in so far as the same were invaded, and they hindered by the bishops." But, by command of Charles the Second, synods,

21

presbyteries, and kirk-sessions had now been (by a proclamation of 9th January 1662) expressly discharged "until they be authorized and ordered by the archbishops and bishops upon their entering unto the government of their respective sees." At his first Diocesan Synod, Sharp took care that ruling elders should have no standing in his presbyteries, or "meetings of the ministers of the respective bounds"; and he likewise circumscribed the power of these "meetings." Instructions were also given that each minister should "assume and choose a competent number of fitt persons, according to the bounds of the parish," to assist in session, etc.

Court of High Commission

Early in 1664 the King resolved to re-erect, by virtue of his royal prerogative, the Court of High Commission, to enforce the Acts "for the peace and order of the Church, and in behalf of the government thereof by archbishops and bishops." The extraordinary power vested in this court was increased in range by the general clause, authorising the Commissioners "to do and execute what they shall find necessary and convenient for his Majesty's service in the premises." Any five of the Commissioners could act, if one of them were an archbishop or bishop. No provision was made for any appeal from the judgment of this court. Of it a learned member of the bar has said: "All law and order were disregarded. The Lord Advocate ceased to act as public prosecutor, and became a member of this iniquitous tribunal. No indictments were required; no defences were allowed; no witnesses were necessary. The accused were dragged before the Commissioners, and compelled to answer any questions which were put to them, without being told of what they were suspected." The court could order ministers "to be censured with suspension or deposition"; and could punish them and others "by fining, confining, committing to prison and incarcerating." For nearly two years this court harassed and oppressed the Nonconformists of Scotland.

Origin of Pentland Rising

Towards the close of 1665, conventicles were, by royal proclamation, forbidden under severe penalties. The officiating ministers, and those harbouring them, were threatened with the highest pains due to sedition, and hearers were subject to fining, confining, and other corporal punishments.

Such measures could hardly be expected to beget in the people an ardent love for Prelacy; and when opposition was manifested in the south-west of Scotland, troops, under Sir James Turner, were sent to suppress it.

Torture and Execution

At length the harshness of a handful of soldiers to an old man, at Dalry in Galloway, led to a scuffle with a few countrymen, and the success of the latter led to the untimely rising which was suppressed by General Dalyell at Rullion

Green on the 28th of November 1666. In that engagement the slain and mortally wounded Covenanters numbered over forty. On the 7th of December ten prisoners—all of whom, save one, had been promised quarter—were hanged at the Market Cross of Edinburgh. In less than a month, fully twenty more prisoners had been hanged at Edinburgh, Glasgow, Irvine, Ayr, and Dumfries. Two of these—Neilson of Corsack and Hugh M'Kail—were tortured in the boots. Never before had drums been used in Scotland to drown the voice of a victim dying on the scaffold. At this time it was introduced at Glasgow.

Had the rising not been so ill-timed, it would probably have been much better supported. After its suppression, Rothes and Dalyell wrote gloomily of the condition of Ayrshire; but Dalyell was not the man to shrink from quelling incipient rebellion by force. Compared with his measures, those of Sir James Turner were mild, although they had driven the sufferers to despair. Finding that his own influence was in peril through the alliance between the military and ecclesiastical party, Lauderdale broke up this brutal administration.

| The Indulgence | The first indulgence (granted in the summer of 1669) was fated, as its successors were, to be a bone of contention among the Covenanters. It was condemned by the more scrupulous because of its restrictions; and because, as they held, compliance with it involved the owning of the royal supremacy in ecclesiastical matters. Many refused to hear the indulged ministers, and some would have nothing to do with those non-indulged ministers who did not denounce the indulgence. It was also disliked and resented by Alexander Burnet, Archbishop of Glasgow, and his diocesan synod, but for very different reasons. They objected to indulged Presbyterian ministers being exempted from Episcopal jurisdiction, and objected all the more because, in some districts, the people would not countenance either doctrine or discipline under Episcopal administration.

| Conventicles | The ejection of the ministers, and the filling of their places by the miserable substitutes then termed "curates," had led to the keeping of conventicles, and as the indulgence, like the proclamation of 1665, failed to put an end to these unauthorised religious services, it was resolved to put them down with a strong hand. Parliament decreed, in 1670, that non-indulged, outed ministers, or other persons not allowed by the bishops, who either preached or prayed in any meeting, "except in ther oune housses and to those of ther oune family," should be deemed guilty of keeping conventicles, and should be imprisoned until they found caution not to do the like again, or bound themselves to leave the kingdom; and those who conducted, or convocated people to, field-conventicles, were to be punished by death and confiscation of their goods,

and hearers were to be severely fined. The Act explained that a house-conventicle became a field-conventicle if there were more persons present than the house contained, so that some of them were outside the door.

That this might not be a dead letter, a reward of five hundred merks was offered to any one who captured a holder of, or convocater to, field-conventicles; and these captors were not to be punished for any slaughter that might be committed in apprehending such delinquents. Even with such a law hanging over their heads, the faithful Covenanters were not prepared to give up their conventicles. The Word of Life was much too precious to be thus parted with. They did not intend, however, to permit the oppressors to drive them or their preachers as lambs to the slaughter, and so they henceforth carried arms for defence.

| Public Worship | As no general attempt had been made, since the Restoration, to alter the services of the Church, save to a very slight degree, the worship of Conformists and Nonconformists was practically the same. Now, however, "many Conformists began to dispute for a liturgy and some to preach for it; but the fox Sharp was not much for it, only because he had no will to ride the ford where his predecessor drowned."

| James Mitchell | An unsuccessful attempt to rid the country of Sharp had been made in 1668 by James Mitchell, who several years afterwards was apprehended; but no proof could be adduced against him, until, on the Lord Chancellor's promise to save his life, he confessed. The Chancellor and Treasurer-Depute swore that they heard him make his confession before the committee; Lauderdale and Sharp swore that they heard him own it before the Privy Council. They denied all knowledge of any promise of life, although the promise had been duly minuted; and the request of Mitchell's advocates, that the Register of the Privy Council should be produced, or the clerks obliged to give extracts, was rejected; and the prisoner was sentenced to be hanged.

In Lord Fountainhall's opinion, this was one of the most solemn criminal trials that had taken place in Scotland for a hundred years; and it was generally believed that the law was strained to secure a conviction. He adds: "It was judged ane argument of a bad deplorat cause that they summoned and picked out ane assysse [i.e., a jury] of souldiers under the King's pay, and others who, as they imagined, would be clear to condemne him." The Privy Council would have granted a reprieve, but Sharp would not consent. On him was laid the chief blame of Mitchell's torture in 1676 and execution in 1678.

| The Ladies' Covenant | According to Dr Hickes, several ladies of great quality, in January 1678, kept a private fast and conventicle in Edinburgh, to ask God to bring to

24

nought the counsels of men against his people; and before they parted they all subscribed a paper, wherein they covenanted, to the utmost of their power, to engage their lords to assist and protect God's people against the devices taken to reduce them to order and obedience. Next month the Highland Host plundered covenanting Ayrshire and Clydesdale.

The Scottish Convention of Estates, professedly
regarding field conventicles as "rendezvouses of
rebellion" with which the ordinary military forces could not successfully cope, and desiring that the "rebellious and schismatick principles may be rooted out by lawfull and sutable means," resolved, in July 1678, to offer the King £1,800,000 Scots, for securing the kingdom against foreign invasion and intestine commotions. The payment was to be spread over five years, and the money raised by five months' cess in each of these years. Many Covenanters denounced the paying of this cess as an active concurring with the Lord's enemies in bearing down his work. Some, however, thought it better to pay than to furnish the unscrupulous collectors with a pretext for destroying their goods, and extorting more than was due. The cess thus became a cause of division, as well as an instrument of oppression.

| The Cess |

The hated Sharp fell into the hands of nine
Covenanters at Magus Muir on the 3rd of May 1679.
Seven of the nine had no misgivings as to what they should do in the circumstances; and they unscientifically butchered him in presence of his servants and daughter. For that deed none were responsible save those who were there; but many were afterwards brought to trouble for it, and not a few, who were perfectly innocent, chose to suffer rather than brand it as murder.

| Sharp's Death |

Some of those who took an active part in the tragedy
of Magus Muir were present at Rutherglen, on
Thursday, the 29th of May, when the bonfires which had been kindled in honour of the King's birthday were extinguished, and when the Act Rescissory and other obnoxious Acts were publicly burned. On Saturday, Claverhouse set out from Glasgow to make some investigations concerning this outrage, and next morning he attempted, but in vain, to disperse an armed conventicle at Drumclog. On this occasion he added nothing to his military reputation; and fled from the field as fast as his wounded charger could carry him. Three weeks later (22nd June 1679) the Covenanters, divided in counsel and badly officered, were slaughtered by hundreds at Bothwell Bridge; and the thousand and more prisoners who were taken were shut up in Greyfriars church-yard, Edinburgh. Some of these prisoners were executed; some escaped; many, after lying for weeks in the open church-yard, were induced to purchase their release by binding themselves never to carry arms against the

| Bothwell Bridge |

King or his authority; and two hundred, after enduring sufferings worse than death, were drowned next December off the coast of Orkney.

Cameronians Donald Cargill and Richard Cameron now became the leaders of the more thorough-going Covenanters —a small and select party as strong in faith as weak in numbers. They were sometimes known as "Cargillites," more commonly as "Cameronians." On the first anniversary of Bothwell Bridge, a score of them rode into Sanquhar, and there emitted a declaration in which they cast off their allegiance to the King, declared war against him, and protested against the succession of James, Duke of York.

The Privy Council replied by offering a reward of five thousand merks for Richard Cameron, dead or alive, and three thousand for his brother or Cargill. On the 22nd of July, both of the Camerons fell at Ayrsmoss; and a year later (27th July 1681) Cargill, who had excommunicated the King and some of the leading persecutors, triumphed over death at the Market Cross of Edinburgh.

Effect of Persecution Those who could not be charged with the breach of any law were asked if they owned the King's authority. If they disowned it, or qualified their acknowledgment, or declined to give their opinion, they were deemed guilty of treason. But, as Alexander Sheilds says: "The more they insisted in this inquisition, the more did the number of witnesses multiply, with a growing increase of undauntedness, so that the then shed blood of the martyrs became the seed of the Church; and as, by hearing and seeing them so signally countenanced of the Lord, many were reclaimed from their courses of complyance, so others were daylie more and more confirmed in the wayes of the Lord, and so strengthened by his grace that they choose rather to endure all torture, and embrace death in its most terrible aspect, than to give the tyrant and his complices any acknowledgment, yea not so much as to say, *God save the King*, which was offered as the price of their life."

The Test On the 31st of August 1681, Parliament passed an "Act anent Religion and the Test." By this Act, every person in public trust or office in Scotland was ordered to take the Test Oath, or be declared incapable of all public trust, and be further punished by the loss of moveables and liferent escheat. By the oath, the swearers bound themselves to adhere to the Confession of Faith of 1560; to disown all principles inconsistent therewith, whether popish or fanatic; to own the King as "the only supream governour of this realme, over all persons and in all causes, as weill ecclesiastical as civill;" to defend all the rights, prerogatives, and privileges of the King, his heirs, and lawful successors; never to enter into covenants or leagues, nor to assemble for consulting or treating in any matter of state, civil or ecclesiastic, without his Majesty's special command or express license; never to take up arms against him or those commissioned by him; never to decline his power and jurisdiction; and they owned that no obligation lay on them by the National Covenant, or by the Solemn League and Covenant, or otherwise, "to endeavour any change or alteration in the government, either in Church or State, as it is now established by the laws of this kingdom." Through the imposing of this complicated Test, many were brought to trouble, and not a few declined it at all hazards.

The Children's Bond — One of the most curious and suggestive documents of this period is known as "The Children's Bond." In 1683, "when there was no faithful minister in Scotland," a number of children in the village of Pentland, who had formed themselves into a society for devotional purposes, solemnly entered into a covenant, of which the following is a copy:—

> "This is a covenant made between the Lord and us, with our whole hearts, and to give up ourselves freely to him, without reserve, soul and body, hearts and affections, to be his children, and him to be our God and Father, if it please the holy Lord to send his Gospel to the land again: that we stand to this covenant, which we have written, between the Lord and us, as we shall answer at the great day; that we shall never break this covenant which we have made between the Lord and us: that we shall stand to this covenant which we have made; and if not, it shall be a witness against us in the great day, when we shall stand before the Lord and his holy angels. O Lord, give us real grace in our hearts to mind Zion's breaches, that is in such a low case this day; and make us to mourn with her, for thou hast said, 'them that mourn with her in the time of her trouble shall rejoice when she rejoiceth, when the Lord will come and bring back the captivity of Zion;' when he shall deliver her out of her enemies' hands, when her King shall come and raise her from the dust, in spite of all her enemies that will oppose her, either devils or men. That thus they have banished her King, Christ, out of the land, yet he will arise and avenge his children's blood, at her enemies' hands, which cruel murderers have shed."

On the back of the document was written:—

> "Them that will not stand to every article of this covenant which we have made betwixt the Lord and us, that they shall not go to the kirk to hear any of these soul-murdering curates, we will neither speak nor converse with them. Any that breaks this covenant they shall never come into our society. We shall declare before the Lord that we

have bound ourselves in covenant, to be covenanted to him all the days of our life, to be his children and him our covenanted Father.

"We subscribe with our hands these presents—

"BETERICK UUMPERSTON.

JANET BROWN.

HELEN MOUTRAY.

MARION SWAN.

JANET SWAN.

ISOBEL CRAIG.

MARTHA LOGAN.

AGNES AITKIN.

MARGARET GALLOWAY.

HELEN STRAITON,

HELEN CLARK.

MARGARET BROWN.

JANET BROWN.

MARION M'MOREN.

CHRISTIAN LAURIE."

| Beatrix Umpherston |

Unfortunately, it is not known who drafted this covenant, nor whether it originated in the spontaneous desire of any of these devout children. Such a child as Emilia Geddie would have been quite competent to frame such a paper. Beatrix Umpherston, whose name heads the list, was then ten years old. She married the Rev. John M'Neil, and died in her ninetieth year.

| The Strategy of Claverhouse |

In a report which Claverhouse gave in this year to the Committee of Privy Council, explaining how he had quietened Galloway, the following passages occur:—

"The churches were quyte desert; no honest man, no minister in saifty. The first work he did was to provyd magasins of corn and strawe in evry pairt of the contry, that he might with conveniency goe with the wholl pairty wherever the King's service requyred; and runing from on place to ane other, nobody could knou wher to surpryse him: and in the mean tyme quartered on the rebelles, and indevoured to distroy them by eating up their provisions; but that they quikly perceived the dessein, and soued their corns on untilled ground. After which, he fell in search of the rebelles, played them hotly with pairtys, so that there wer severall taken, many fleid the contry, and all wer dung from their hants; and then rifled so their houses, ruined their goods, and imprisoned their servants, that their wyfes and schildring were broght to sterving; which forced them to have recours to the saif conduct, and made them glaid to renounce their principles…. He ordered the colecttors of evry parish to bring in exact rolls, upon oath, and atested by the minister; and caused read them evry Sunday after the first sermon, and marque the absents; who wer severly punished if obstinat. And wherever he heard of a parish that was considerably behynd, he went thither on Saturday, having aquainted them to meet, and asseured them he would be present at sermon; and whoever was absent on Sunday was punished on Monday; and who would not apear either at church or court, he caused arest there goods, and then offer them saif conduct: which broght in many, and will bring in all, and actually broght in tuo outed disorderly ministers."

| The Success of Claverhouse |

So this booted apostle of Episcopacy confessedly caused men to renounce their principles by driving them from their haunts, rifling their houses, ruining their goods, imprisoning their servants, and bringing their wives and children to starvation! And so he filled the deserted churches by causing an attested roll to be read every Sabbath after the first sermon, and severely punishing the absentees, if obstinate. In extreme cases he even attended church himself, and those who were absent on Sabbath were dealt with on Monday. But, ere long, measures much more severe were to be adopted.

| Apologetic Declaration |

The devout and gentle but resolute Renwick, having been sent to Holland for ordination, returned in the autumn of 1683 to the arduous and dangerous post which had been so honourably held by Cameron and Cargill, and they could not have had a worthier successor. In November 1684, the Cameronians published their "Apologetick Declaration and Admonitory Vindication," in which they adhered to their former declarations against Charles Stuart, and warned those who sought their lives or gave information against them, that in future they would regard them as the enemies of God and of the covenanted work of reformation, and would punish them as such. The Privy Council met this declaration by ordaining that those who owned it, or would not disown it upon oath, should be immediately put to death whether they had arms or not.

This was to be always done "in presence of two witnesses, and the person or

The Killing-time persons having commission from the Council for that effect." The darkest time of the persecution, the period specially known as "the killing-time," had now arrived; prisoners had already been hurried to death three hours after receiving sentence.

The infamous Lauderdale had been constrained to demit his office in 1680, and his life in 1682; Rothes had predeceased him by a year; and now they were to be followed into another world by the crowned scoundrel (otherwise "His most Sacred Majesty") for whose favour they had persecuted the followers of that cause which all three had sworn to maintain. By the death of Charles the Second, on the 6th of February 1685, no relief came to those who were hunted like partridges on the hills of Scotland.

Priesthill and
Wigtown The heartless sensualist was now to be succeeded by him who combined unrelenting bigotry with lechery. Charles had long been suspected of more than secret leanings to the Church of Rome; James was an avowed and ardent Papist. It was on the 1st of the following May that, under Claverhouse, the dread scene was enacted at Priesthill, when John Brown was taken to his own door, and shot in presence of his wife and child; and on the 11th of the same month that this cold-blooded cruelty was rivalled by Lag at Wigtown, when Margaret Wilson and Margaret Lauchlison (or M'Lauchlan) were tied to stakes and drowned by the rising tide.

Conventicles Between these two tragedies, the Scottish Parliament of the new King distinguished itself by passing three harsh Acts. One of these declared it treason to give or take the Covenants, to write in defence of them, or to own them as lawful or binding; the second declared the procedure of the Privy Council to have been legal in fining husbands "for their wives withdrawing from the ordinances"; and by the other the penalty of death and confiscation of goods was adopted as the punishment to be inflicted on hearers as well as on preachers at either house or field conventicles. Yet even with this stringent Act it was impossible to put down conventicles. It was not for the mere satisfaction of opposing a tyrannical and bloodthirsty Government that the frequenters of conventicles were willing to risk so much. Renwick's sermons show that he was a faithful preacher of the Gospel; and those who had realised in their own experience that it was the power of God unto salvation were anxious at all hazards to listen to the Word when proclaimed by such a devoted and fearless messenger.

Dunnottar Prisoners In order to cope more successfully with the expected rising of the Earl of Argyll, 184 captive Covenanters, collected from various prisons, were, in May 1685, marched from Burntisland to Dunnottar. A few escaped by the way. The others suffered a rigorous and cruel imprisonment. For several days they were, male and female, confined in a single vault, dark, damp, and unfurnished. During the course of the summer some escaped, some died, some took the obnoxious oaths. Of those who were brought back to Leith and examined before the Privy Council, on the 18th of August, a considerable number were already under sentence of banishment, and now 51 men and 21 women were similarly sentenced, and forbidden to return to Scotland, without special permission, under pain of death.

| The Toleration | Argyll's rising was a failure. He was captured, brought to Edinburgh, and there beheaded on the 30th of June 1685, not for the rising, but because in November 1681 he had ventured to take the Test with an explanation. Being dissatisfied with Argyll's Declaration and with his associates, Renwick and his followers stood aloof from that rising; but, on the 28th of May 1685, they had, at Sanquhar, formally protested against the validity of the Scottish Parliament then in session, and also against the proclamation of James, Duke of York, as King. They also refused to take any benefit from the toleration, which he granted, by his "sovereign authority, prerogative royal, and absolute power," on the 28th of June 1687—a toleration which was gratefully accepted by many of the less scrupulous Presbyterian ministers. Although Argyll's attempt to overturn the throne of James the Seventh was unsuccessful, the time came, in December 1688, when he had to escape from the country, which was no longer to be his. Next April the Scottish Convention of Estates pointed out that he had assumed the regal power in Scotland, and acted as king, without taking the oath required by law, whereby the king is obliged to swear to maintain the Protestant religion, and to rule the people according to the laws.

| The Revolution | Renwick, who glorified God in the Grassmarket on the 17th of February 1688, was the last Covenanter who suffered on a scaffold. He and his followers, by maintaining an unflinching protest against the reign of James, had helped to hasten his downfall. When the Convention of Estates met in Edinburgh, the Cameronians gladly volunteered to defend it; and showed their loyalty by raising in a single day, without tuck of drum, eleven hundred and forty men as a regiment for King William's service.

Episcopacy was abolished by the Scottish Parliament (22nd July 1689) as an insupportable grievance; and (7th June 1690) Presbytery was re-established, and the Westminster Confession of Faith ratified; but the Covenants were ignored, and on that account the sterner Cameronians still stood apart, and, with that dogged tenacity which had distinguished them in the past, they held together, although for many long years they had no minister.

The Martyrs'
Monument On the Martyrs' Monument in the Greyfriars
Churchyard, Edinburgh, it is stated that, between
Argyll's execution and Renwick's, there "were one way or other murdered
and destroyed for the same cause about eighteen thousand." This estimate is
Estimated Number
of Victims not given upon the original monument, erected in
1706 through the instrumentality of James Currie
(Beatrix Umpherston's stepfather), and now preserved in the interesting and
well-appointed Municipal Museum in the Edinburgh Corporation Buildings.
That monument was repaired, and a compartment added to it, in 1728 or
1729; and the present monument supplanted it in or about 1771. The estimate
has apparently been taken from Defoe's "Memoirs of the Church of
Scotland," first published in 1717. It therefore includes those who went into
exile, those who were banished, those who died from hunger, cold, and
disease contracted in their wanderings, and those who were killed in battle, as
well as those who were murdered in the fields or executed with more
formality. The numbers which he sets down under some of these classes are
only guesses, and seem to be rather wild guesses. An estimate approaching
more closely to the real number might be made, and would doubtless show a
much smaller, though still a surprisingly large, total. But the exact number of
those who laid down their lives, in that suffering, or heroic, period of the
Church of Scotland, will not be known until the dead, small and great, stand
before God, and the Book of Life is opened. Of many of them no earthly
record remains.

"The shaggy gorse and brown heath wave

O'er many a nameless warrior's grave."

Heroic Sufferers Not a few of the sufferers endured torments more
terrible than death. Some were tortured with fire-
matches, which permanently disabled their hands; some had their thumbs
mercilessly squeezed in the thumbikins; some had their legs horribly bruised
in the boots; and some were kept awake by watchful soldiers for nine
consecutive nights. It is not surprising that nervous, sensitive men
occasionally shrunk back in the day of trial. The wonder is that so many stood
firm.

Lightning Source UK Ltd.
Milton Keynes UK
UKHW040310101120
R2506300001B/R25063PG372410UKX1B/1